T0365367

CHOCOLATE CHIP MORSELS

Short Stories for the Child in You

PSALMA MAMA a.k.a. Dawn Gwin

WestBow Press books may be ordered through booksellers or by contacting:

WestBow Press
A Division of Thomas Nelson & Zondervan
1663 Liberty Drive
Bloomington, IN 47403
www.westbowpress.com
1 (866) 928-1240

ISBN: 978-1-4908-5638-4 (sc)
ISBN: 978-1-4908-5639-1 (e)

Library of Congress Control Number: 2014918894

Printed in the United States of America.

WestBow Press rev. date: 12/3/2014

WESTBOW
PRESS
A DIVISION OF THOMAS NELSON
& ZONDERVAN

Contents

Chocolate Chip Morsels

I can think about a homemade apple pie baking in the oven with its fresh sliced apples, cinnamon and nutmeg, with melted butter and filling drizzling over the sides, and can almost smell it, even taste it. Can you?

Or how about crispy chicken fried up in a pan?

Or, a big pot of hot chocolate simmering on the stove, waiting for the marshmallows to go in?

Yum! I have fond memories from each of these, but none as good as the smell of my Mom's chocolate chip cookies. When walking home from school, I can smell them baking in the oven, ready to come out, as I walk up the driveway.

My brother, Reagan loves Mama's cookies so much, that when Mama asked him what he wanted for his birthday last year, Reagan told her he just wanted some of her chocolate chip cookies, and that's just what he got too. Reagan ate cookies that day and drank milk with them till I thought his stomach would explode.

One of our favorite things Mama does before mixing the dough for the cookies is, she passes out three chocolate chip morsels to each of us four kids before she pours the rest into the mixing bowl. Yep! We get three morsels each.

One day after school, I came in and Mama told me to put my backpack in my room; but I heard her from the kitchen and knew she must be making us something good, and I was hungry, so I just slung my backpack anywhere. It landed on the other side of the couch where my little brother John was laying, but I didn't know it till John jumped up, and went crying to Mama and told her I threw my backpack and hit him on his face on purpose.

Mama was passing out chocolate chip morsels about that time, and skipped right over me. I told Mama it was an accident, and told John I was very sorry it hit him; but Mama sent me to my room for disobeying her. "Kayla" she said, you'll have to miss out on the morsels this time." I ran to my room, threw myself on my bed and cried.

In a few minutes, Little John came in my room and although he barely stood tall enough, he got on his tippy toes and put something on top of my desk, and said, "I love you Sissy" as he ran out.

When I dried my tears so I could peek over and see what John left, I cried even harder when I saw his three little chocolate chip morsels he had left for me. That act of love spoke so loud to me! Before, I had been crying because I felt sorry for myself that I didn't get the morsels, and missed out on Mama's blessing. Now I was crying because I disobeyed Mom, and because little brother lost out by giving his morsels to me. I was now sad for the fact my wrong action caused little brother to miss out.

In Sunday School, they taught us Jesus had everything He would ever need in Heaven; but He chose to come to earth, and give it all to us. Just like my little brother John giving me his morsels when I didn't deserve it, Jesus gave all His morsels to us that the Father gave Him, even though we don't deserve it. That is so sweet of Him!!! When Mama bakes chocolate chip cookies for us, she tells us that when we speak kind words to each other, it is like giving away a yummy chocolate chip morsel each time we do. Then, Mama tells us that's why we have the Bible; because "Jesus wants to pour His Words in to us. It is like our heart is the mixing bowl, and His Words are sweet chocolate chip morsels being poured in to us." I thanked Jesus for sharing His chocolate chip morsels from Heaven with us, and with me!

What morsels are you leaving today for others?

The End

A Gift For Mama

A boy knew his Mama loved to eat frog legs
and it was her birthday today,
so he found his bucket to catch all he could,
and then went on his way.
The boy filled the bucket to the rim;
then a Frog peeked up and YELLED at him,

"Your chances of keeping us in here are slim:
Wouldn't you rather take home a Duck**?"**

"Now, why" said the boy, "would I want a Duck?"
Frog said, "A Duck would bring good luck!"
So the boy let the Frogs hop back to the lake:
and just as he did he knew it was a mistake.
But he looked up and spotted a beautiful Drake;
(a Drake is a boy duck, by the way.)

The boy ran home and got his rod and reel,
and caught that Ducky by the bill.

While walking home with the feathery fowl, Duck said,
"Say boy, wouldn't you rather have a Cow?"

"A Cow would give you lots of milk; but I would be good for only one meal.

Ooo, but a Cow... WOW! What a deal!
Your Mom would be so proud of you.
Instead of a Quack why not take home a *Moo*?!"

So the boy let the Duck go and said, "So long Drake!"
Right when he did he knew it was a mistake.
He looked up and saw a Cow drinking from the lake;

then he was on his way.
The boy and the Cow went around and around
until he finally got that ole' heifer to sit down.

He couldn't lift the bucket now and the Cow just laughed,

and said, "Wouldn't you rather take home a Giraffe?"
"Your Mama loves to see them in the Zoo
and she would be so proud of you!"
So the boy let the Cow go back to the lake
and hoped he hadn't made another mistake.
The boy went far to find a Giraffe from a Zoo.
When the Giraffe saw the bucket, he laughed too.

"Surely you don't think I could fit in *there*!"
The boy went over and plopped down in a chair:
He told the Giraffe where all he had been.
The Giraffe stayed there and listened to him.

"My Mama likes frog legs so I filled my bucket up –
with lots of Frogs who told me I should get a *Duck*."

So I let the Frogs go and caught my Mama a Duck
just because the Frogs said it would bring good luck.
I had no luck at all, just a feathery fowl
who said I'd be much better off with a *Cow*.
I let the Duck go, then the Cow wouldn't fit... here in my bucket not one bit.
Then the Cow told me I needed a *Giraffe*.
I found one but all you can do is laugh!
So what do I do now, Mercy Sakes?!
By now I've made a whole bunch of mistakes!"

The Giraffe bent down with his long tall neck
and said, "Looks like Boy you're going to have to go back!"
"If you had taken the frog legs to your Mama back then,
she could have had them for lunch fried up in a pan.
But hop up here on my head, and I'll show you the sights:
I'll even take you home from here if you like."

"You can be thinking while you're on my head,
what you can do for your Mama since it's her birthday you said."
When the Mama saw her Son riding on the Giraffe,
she threw her head back and she laughed and she laughed!

The boy slid down the Giraffe's long tall neck
and picked up such speed that when he
slid off its back,
He flew through the air about a mile or so,
and landed in a frog pond down below.
While he was there he had such a ball,
and Mama got her frog legs after all!

The End

The Moral of the story is: Sometimes GOD speaks to you through other people. Other times, He speaks directly to your heart. It is important to learn to follow the right voice, or else you may find yourself listening to a giraffe.

Butter Your Own Corn

Robert was the only child until his little brother, Rubert was born.

Robert was four years old, and helped out a lot with his little brother. He fed him his bottle, played with him, and helped him fall asleep; but he didn't change Rubert's stinky diapers. When Rubert got to be about four years old himself, he was so used to having help with all he did. Since he always had his older brother Robert do everything for him, Rubert just got to where he expected Robert to. Rubert let everyone else do all the work, because he didn't know any better.

Robert saw little Rubert was not growing up, so he decided to help him do so. Mama put corn on the cob on everyone's plate that night for supper. Rubert handed his plate to his older brother and said, "Here, butter this!" Robert passed the plate back to Rubert and said, "Butter your own corn!"

From then on, when Robert saw Rubert could do something himself, he would tell him those same words, "Butter your own corn little brother!" Rubert would throw a little fit, and Robert just ignored his little brother when he would throw himself on the floor and cry.

Next time Mama fixed corn on the cob and put it on the boy's plates, Rubert picked up his brother's cob and threw it across the room and just laughed, as he yelled, ***"Doe dedit, and butter your own torn Bubba!"***

(which meant, "Go get it, and butter your own corn Bubba!")

From then on, the family used this line often, to get their point across. Robert was eight years old now. He had a temptation to be on the lazy side once in a while. One night, after supper dishes were put up, Mama told Robert to go empty the trash. Robert tried to put it off by pretending that he didn't hear his Mama's instructions. He immediately went to the living room and started playing his game. Mama went to throw something away and noticed her son hadn't done what she said.

"Robert, get in here and empty this trash right now." Mama said. "Then you can play your game." After seeing what a mess he had to clean up off the floor around the trash can, and how full it was, Robert asked his Mom, "Will you help me take out the trash?" His Mama replied, "Did you need help playing that game in there?" "No Ma'am" he said, shyly.

Then Mama replied, "You can do it yourself, I've got my work to do." Mama waited till Robert was on the way out the door with the trash bag, then called his name, "Robert?" Robert stopped and looked over at her; she smiled and said, *"Butter your own corn!"*

That made them both laugh.

That fall, when the boys started back to school, Robert's Teacher asked her students to "Write a story about something that happened in the summer." Robert wrote the story about the corn on the cob and how Rubert was growing up and learning to do things on his own now. Rubert missed being coddled and spoiled; but even Rubert realized later on, his older brother must have loved him a whole lot to stand back and stop doing things for him that he should do himself.

One night Robert didn't study for the next day's test at school, and when it got to a question Robert didn't know, he found himself looking over at a friend's paper for the answer.

Teacher looked up just in time to see Robert cheating on the test and she could have really embarrassed him. Instead, his Teacher thought of the story Robert had written at the first of the year, and called his name: "Robert!" the Teacher exclaimed.

Stunned and embarrassed he had been caught, Robert with shamed-face looked up at his Teacher, knowing he was probably about to be thought bad of by the whole class: "Yes Ma'am?" Robert replied. Teacher just smiled and said to him,

"Butter your own corn!"

Robert looked puzzled, because he wondered how she knew the phrase his family used at home often. Then he remembered the story he had shared with the class at the beginning of the school year.

Robert was so relieved and thankful his Teacher hadn't let the entire class know what he'd done! He smiled back at his Teacher as if to say "Thank you!" but again answered, "Yes Ma'am."

The Moral of this story is: Sometimes you need help, and need to ask for it when you do. Other times, you would just get lazy if you didn't do certain things yourself. Sometimes you just need to step up and *"Butter your own corn!"*

The End

New Best Friend

When he was two years old, he was found.
The Dog Catcher caught him and took him to the Pound.
His hair was all knotted; he had stickers in one foot:
The Dog Catcher told him he was "Just an ole' mutt!"
"Come on Mutt!" he said, and locked him away:
For a long time that is where "Mutt" stayed.
Day after day and year after year,
many people would go by there,
Looking to adopt a pet of their own.
Would they pick him? Would they take him home?

Mutt stood tall when people walked by,
wagging his tail, and hoped they'd give him a try.
From time to time someone would ask,

"Dog Catcher, what kind of dog is this?"
Dog Catcher would make an awful face, and say,
"O, he's just a mutt, the ugliest one in this place."
Then he'd say, "If you're looking for a good family pet,
don't pick him: he's just a mutt, don't forget."
It got to where, when people came by
to pick out a pet, Mutt would hide.
He would go lay down at the back of his cage, and
stay there with his tail between his legs.
He thought the other animals were much cuter than him,
and he could tell people really wanted them.

It was hurting Mutt's health, he was even shrinking in size;
Because he had been rejected so many times.

Then a man came by one day to the Pound,
"I need a "Man's best friend!" he said, "You got one around?"
The kind man picked his favorite one in the place:
The Dog Catcher laughed and said, "You've made a mistake:
This dog is good for nothing: he won't do!
I'll pick out a better one for you!"
The kind man insisted on taking "Mutt" home:
"I've made my choice" he said, "leave me alone!"

Mutt got a bath and stood up tall.
His owner said,
"Well now! You're not a mutt after all!"
"I am changing your name. You like the name, "Best Friend?"
The man hugged his dog and said, "I'll never let anyone abuse you again!!"

The Dog Catcher at the Pound was an awful deceiver
But it turns out, the "Mutt"
was a GOLDEN RETRIEVER!

The End

The Moral of the story is: You are Important, a one of a kind, no matter how you see yourself, or how you think others see you. Others may label you as, "nothing but a mutt;" but don't you believe it! You are here for a reason: GOD's reason. GOD designed you on purpose, for His purpose. He made you in His Own Image, His Likeness. If you have made wrong choices that got you into trouble... still, guess what? GOD saw your purpose from the beginning of time and He knows what you're really capable of. Follow Him, walking in Love at every chance, and you will see His purpose for you too.

He will even give YOU a new name.

The Day I Met GOD

I am excited to tell you about the most wonderful day of my life: the day I met GOD, our Creator.

I was a child who loved sports, but couldn't play them too much because of asthma. I would get out of breath so easily, but wanted to keep going anyway. It would sure get me in trouble with my health when I did too much though. I remember in about third grade when I jumped rope to a nonsense rhyme: "Cinderella, dressed in yella went upstairs to kiss her fella: made a mistake and kissed a snake, how many Dr.'s did it take? It took 1-2-3-4....20-21-22" and so on. I jumped so many times, I fainted. I remember waking up at home with pink sheets on my bed.

I wanted to please my parents in many ways, but I also did things I wasn't supposed to. I lied sometimes to get out of things. I stole doll clothes from a neighborhood girl, and a Barbie Doll telephone one time I think.

Later on in years, I was suffering in my health even more. I missed out on so many things other children could do that I couldn't. I remember climbing to the top of my brother's bunk bed so I could watch my brothers and sister play in the snow. I played with them outside, but would get tired before they did and would have to go in.

I would let things get me down quite often growing up. I could have made better grades if I had tried harder, and kept my mind on my school work, but instead I thought too much about other things. One thing I thought a lot about is, music. I spent much of my time memorizing words to songs that I liked. Some of my favorite groups were the Beatles, Three Dog Night, Diana Ross, Dionne Warwick, The Lettermen, The Beach Boys, and too many others to number. I still like to listen to different styles of music, as long as they have words that feed me good thoughts about myself, and others. Especially if they cheer me up, and encourage me to be all I can be. I love songs about Jesus because He has done so very much for me!

I told you how much my health suffered, and how I had gotten depressed. I also had a problem in my life that I tried so hard to stop doing, but couldn't. I couldn't talk to anyone about it, and would get spankings many times for it, but I just couldn't stop, no matter what I tried. My secret problem was, that I wet the bed. I would try not drinking for a couple of hours before going to sleep... that didn't work. I tried staying awake, so I wouldn't go to sleep and make this big mistake again, but that wasn't happening either. I was a very hard sleeper. I would have these accidents in the bed several nights a week, which added to my sadness. It was like having a big wart on the end of your nose and not being able to do a thing about it.

Later in years I was in a bad car wreck that caused blood clots in my left leg. The clots travelled to my kidney, then to my lungs.

The doctor wanted to put some kind of balloon in my lungs in an operation. I was afraid it would cost my family a lot of money they did not have. I didn't know what to do.

Then something wonderful happened! I met GOD.

I'll explain: Someone came over to buy our birds because they saw the ad in the newspaper. We had two cockatiel birds, one named Percy, the other Pearl. We were trying to make money any honest way we could. I asked the woman who bought them if I could visit them someday. She smiled and said I could. The kind woman noticed I was hurting from pain in my body and asked me the strangest question I ever heard. "Do you know GOD?" she asked. I told her I didn't, then she explained to me about how she met GOD a long time ago, and has been so happy since then. She told me I could know Him too if I just ask Him. After she left, I did what the woman said: I went and sat down and felt very silly doing so, but did it anyway. I said something like, "Dear GOD, I don't know if You can hear me. You are probably busy with a bunch of people and other stuff but that woman told me You could heal me, and she also said I could know You, so will You show me how to know You please?

O, and if You really can heal me, will You do that too please?"

I did not expect anything to happen, but right after I got to sleep that night, I felt like a garden hose was spraying from the top of my head, all through my body and out my feet, like something washed out a bunch of yucky stuff. I don't know how else to describe it. I knew GOD healed me. I knew it was Him... not sure how, but I knew He healed me that night. The doctor checked me and said I didn't have any blood clots in my left leg anymore.

Something else happened the night GOD healed me. He revealed Himself to me that way, but He also allowed me to feel something deep inside, like in the deepest part of me.

What I mean is, the place where I had cried the hardest. It was like, GOD touched the pain I had inside from things I never talked about. For instance, when they picked people to be on a team at school, and I was afraid to be picked last; or when I felt like girls were laughing and talking about me because I didn't have nice clothes like they did. Or, when a boy I liked was nice to me when his friends weren't around, but would tease me and make fun of me when his friends were there. That place deep inside my thoughts is where GOD touched me that night.

I knew right then He loved me. He hears me even when I don't speak out loud. He hears my happy thoughts, my sad thoughts, my wrong thoughts, my right thoughts. He knows everything about me.

After He revealed Himself to me, I asked Him if He would speak to me. I didn't know what else to do, but I thought of going and getting a Bible out of the bookcase. I never could understand what it said, but this time it was different. I didn't know where to turn, so I just opened it anywhere. It fell open right where I needed it to, which told me GOD even took control of that.

My Bible fell open to Romans Chapter 10, verses 9 & 10 It says, "If you will confess with your mouth Jesus is Lord, and believe in your heart GOD raised Him from the dead, you will be saved." I had NO IDEA what any of that meant, I just did it. I said,

"Uhh, well… okay, I say out loud, Jesus is Lord. Do I believe GOD raised Him from the dead? I guess so… if You say so. Okay, I believe it. So now I'll be saved, but from what?" I asked Him.

All of a sudden GOD showed me my heart and everything I had ever done wrong. When I lied, when I cheated at school, when I stole stuff, when I was disobedient to my parents, when I talked bad about someone behind their back. Lots of things came to me that I had done wrong, and things I had said to hurt someone. I apologized to GOD and told Him I was real sorry for all those things, and I named them one by one, just like He showed me, one thing at a time. I felt like I had a big bubble bath on the inside of my heart. I felt so clean and so happy, and so forgiven for everything I had ever done wrong. GOD forgave me that day, and He cleaned my heart so good. After that, He started teaching me from the Bible and from other people how to know Him better. It is so easy to *want to* make Him happy, but sometimes I forget and want my own way. GOD has helped me through tons of stuff and even took away my sadness and sickness. I still get sad and sick at times, and make wrong choices sometimes, but GOD helps me and points me in the right direction, and teaches me from His Words in the Bible to think right. He gave me a new incredible gift to be able to write songs, and poems, and stories like this one for people, to help them know Him too. I love Him, and my life with Him here on earth. Someday I get to go be with Him and see Him in Heaven, and everyone who follows Jesus will be there too. I can't hardly wait to see my Grandmother and Grandpa who are there already. And I can't hardly wait to meet Jesus Who died for me on the Cross and took the punishment I deserve for my sins. I also want to meet David from the Bible, and find out how big that giant really was, and what it was like to trust GOD and take that giant down. I can hardly wait to see the angels either. I bet they are HUGE. I always wanted to know if they play hopscotch and other games on the clouds, so I look forward to asking them. I hope you will meet GOD too so you can follow Jesus and be there with me. We could be good friends in Heaven.

O, one more thing: I forgot to tell you something. Remember the agonizing problem I had at night because I was such a sound sleeper? Since the day I met GOD, I have never once had that problem again. He is so sweet and kind!

The End

Will You Marry Me?

There is something I have thought about all of my life.

When I was a little girl I would always dream
that a Prince on a white horse would someday marry me
and in my imagination I would always pretend
that this Prince would love me O so much
and His love would never end.
And it would be so easy for me to love my Prince too
for you see, He would overlook my every fault, and help me through them too.

Then I went through adolescence and O how hard it was
just trying to fit in some place, even with all my silly thoughts and ways.
Oh I was still that little girl with the same old dream
But I saw no signs of my Prince, and I knew no King.
I was hurting O so bad; my heart was full of sin:
Not a very good time to meet a Prince
when you're dirty and feel ugly within.

Then I met a lady and she invited me to her church and I went
They were singing and praying and I felt like something would be Heaven sent
Then all of a sudden the church doors flew open.....and so did my heart.
It was the Prince of Glory and He was riding on a white horse
When He rode in, He was looking right at me.... at ME!
He rode right up to me and do you know what He said?
He said, "I've loved you since you were a little girl;
I was in your dream.
I was that Prince on the white horse!
Will you marry Me?"

Under GOD's Love

You can't teach a lion to put on underwear;

You can't teach an elephant to sit lightly in a chair;
You can't expect your boxer pup to put on gloves;

And you can't get out from under GOD'S LOVE!

You can't give an ice-cream cone just one lick;

You sure can't hop just one time on a pogo-stick;

You can't have one Hug, and say you've had enough;

And you can't get out from under GOD's LOVE!

You can't teach a kitty-cat not to meow;

You can't take the moo right out of a cow;

You can't take the sky down from above;
And you can't get out from
under GOD's LOVE!

Now, you might try to get your skunk not to stink;
You might can get your orangutan to skate at the rink;

You can try to get your iguana to use a Sippy Cup;
But you can't get out from under GOD's LOVE!

GOD can love you wherever you go: No matter how fast you move, or how slow.
GOD can see you as He sees each star & GOD knows
exactly why you're the way you are.
He can see you when you're happy! He can see you when you're sad!
God can see when you are naughty, or when you act good or bad.
But there is just one thing He cannot do:
GOD can't forget about His LOVE FOR YOU!!

The End
Story illustrations by 12 year old Erin Olivia Otts

Don't Stop Hoping

Once upon a time there was
a caterpillar full of fuzz:
He knew one day he would fly,
so he didn't fret as the days went by.
He also knew that he'd be pretty,
so he didn't fear, not an itty-bitty.
He spun himself a fine cocoon;
then found himself to have no room.
GOD knew the caterpillar would be at his best
only after he went thru some test:
So He hung him in a tree upside down,
and kept him there till the sun went down.

The caterpillar sure didn't want to be
hanging out alone in a big oak tree:

But, even though he didn't understand, he trusted
GOD had a perfect plan.
He cried all night but then come morn,
that fuzzy little worm was no longer forlorn
because Jesus answered that little worm's cry,
and made him a beautiful butterfly.
So wait a little longer, after you've done all you can.
Don't stop hoping, for GOD has got a plan for you.
Just wait a little longer: Jesus **will** come through.
He's making YOU beautiful too!

The End

Stolen Roses

When one parent raises a child alone, they both grow up together.

Ella and her son, Scott were very close. Scott was a bright ten year old boy who was likeable, friendly, and pleasant to be around. His Mom owned and operated a flower shop and loved working there. Scott liked riding his bike over to his Mom's work after school, many times when he could join her in delivering bouquets to surprise people. He and his Mom had lots of good things happen when they delivered flowers.

The most shocking response they ever had, and funny too, was while delivering a beautiful daisy arrangement to this one woman. The woman cried when she opened her door and saw her flowers. When the woman's little three year old girl saw the florist had made her Mama cry, she got mad and kicked Ella real hard right in the shin. Ella walked away limping a little, while her and Scott laughed. They would replay this story often, to stir up conversation with others.

Another memory Scott and Ella brought up often was the time they delivered a rather expensive and very large assortment of flowers to a woman who shouted with glee when she got the knock on her door from the florist. That day, Scott asked if he could please be the one to give the flowers, so his Mom said he could. She walked up the sidewalk with him as he handed the flowers to the very happy woman. There wasn't a card with the flowers. Ella explained to the woman it was because a card wasn't ordered with the flowers. The woman receiving the arrangement smiled even brighter and said, "Oh, a card is not necessary. I sent these to myself to cheer up my day!" They all laughed and as the two walked away, Scott's Mom said to him, "Son, it takes all kinds to make the world go around. You will find that out soon enough."

Scott and his Mom had an agreement at dinner. She would do the meat if he would chop up the vegetables. It worked out fine that way. After dinner, Mama would read a Bible story and they would discuss it afterward about what they could do differently in their lives from the lesson they learned. Bedtime was always fun, because they would tell the same Bible story they had read earlier, only this time in their own words. Both of them took turns retelling the story. Sometimes Scott would get a little mixed up. For instance, one night he was telling his Mama all about how an Angel kept the lions' mouths shut while David was getting his sling shot ready to wipe out the giant.

They had many good laughs. One evening, Scott said, "Hey Mama! Does the Bible say anything about squirrels?" Mama couldn't remember if it did or not. "I know! How about we make up a story about a squirrel?" he said. Then he added, "You want to go first?" That started a bunch of nights of them telling stories to each other. The first night Mama said something like, "Uh... well, once upon a time there lived a squirrel named Chatterbox who was always chattering about this and that. He especially loved it when it would rain, because...." Then his Mom would turn the story over to Scott who would say something like, "Ohh, and uhh... Chatterbox liked to play in the rain because it would make the tree very slippery like a slippery slide and he taught all his friends to slide down the tree.

When they got to the bottom of the tree, they would…" Then it was Mama's turn again. She laughed and finished the story. She said, "And each time they would get to the bottom of the tree, they would go CLUNK! The end." They loved their made-up stories, and also the Bible stories very much, because it made them go to sleep happy!

One day Scott didn't ride his bike to his Mom's flower shop after school, because she called and told him to ride his bike home instead. When Scott got home, he heard his Mama crying. She held him as she told him the news she got from her doctor that day. The doctor told her she had a very bad sickness that would require her to stop working right away, or else it would take too much strength from her. Ella tried to be strong for her son, but she was so shocked by the news herself she couldn't hold back her tears.

That night, they skipped the Bible story. That was too bad, because GOD's words would have helped them. The two of them fell asleep early due to all the stress and them crying and all. In the middle of the night, Scott woke up crying from a nightmare he had. Mama came in and held Scott and prayed with him. When he calmed down, he rolled over toward his nightstand to go to sleep. Mama thought he was asleep so she started to slip out, but Scott asked, "Mom?" "Yes darling," Mama replied. Scott asked, "Is your face pointing toward me?" Ella could hardly speak, but swallowed hard and answered, "Yes, my face is pointing toward you… now go to sleep son." When he did, his Mama slipped into her bedroom got on her knees beside her bed and cried, "Father GOD, I have to know something! Is Your Face pointing toward me?" She knew the answer was yes because He comforted her heart.

Ella's favorite flower was a rose, and Scott knew it. On his way home from school, he saw so many rose bushes in several different yards. He didn't see any harm with picking one rose a day; so every day after school, Scott would pluck one rose and bring it home to his Mama.

Some days it was a red rose, other days a white, or pink, or yellow rose. Sometimes the owners of the rose bush would step out on their porch to let the boy know he had been seen. The boy was hurting inside about his Mama. He wasn't thinking about whether or not he was doing the right thing.

The day after his nightmare, Scott returned home and handed his Mama her rose; then he went to his room to change into his play clothes. He noticed a picture frame on his nightstand beside his bed, the one he always faced while going to sleep. Happy tears came to his eyes when he saw his Mama's picture in the frame, letting him know her face would always point toward his.

Ella and Scott prayed and asked GOD to let her live long enough to finish raising him, and to let her get to know Scott's wife when he grows up and gets married.

That night, Ella added to her prayer, "And Father, I ask You do this, not for me but so Scott and I can tell people how good You have been to us. How You answered our prayers, just because You are good and love us. In Jesus' Name, Amen."

Pretty soon after that, Ella was regaining her strength back. Scott knew it was only because of the prayer they had prayed and that GOD was answering, "Yes." Ella told her son, "Since summer is here, you and I need to think of a really good hobby to do together, so I can keep gaining strength and get back to the flower shop." Scott thought and thought, "Hmm, I wonder what we could do?" His Mom looked into her son's eyes very lovingly and said to him, "I think I know. Son, what do you think about you and I going and buying some rose bushes in different colors, planting them in our yard, watching them grow; then we could go and deliver them to all the people you took roses from?" Scott gasped! "Uh... well, uh... O man Mom! You knew they were stolen roses?" Ella replied, "Yes my sweet son, of course I did."

Now tears were streaming down both of their faces as Scott asked, "Then why didn't you ever give me a spanking?" Mom took her son by both hands and with compassion in her voice said, "Because, I knew why you were taking them." She added, "But it still wasn't right and we must return them to their rightful owners. You will need to apologize to each person you stole them from, okay?" Scott agreed. "I will be happy to." "O, hey Mom! I just had an idea. While we are taking roses to the one's I owe them to, how about we take some to that woman who sent those flowers to herself last summer?"

The End

Why Won't You Be Kind Porcupine

Once upon a time there lived a porcupine.

He had sharp little arrows up and down his spine.

Some called him "Pokey Pokey;" others named him, Spike!

Because he even shot arrows at the one's he liked.

He shot his neighbors, Tooty-Tooty Raccoon,

And even Turtle Shelly, every morning, night, and noon.

Whenever Tooty-Tooty or Shelly would come close, Spike would puff up everywhere but his nose.

He guarded himself with his sharp little hairs, from Wolverines, Coyotes, Lions, and Bears…

Yes……….. even BIG Bears!

But, he also protected himself from those

Who would be a good friend if he would let them get close.

Spike didn't want to get anyone scared; and wouldn't have hurt them if he'd known they cared. He didn't know HOW to be a friend. He was lonely but didn't know HOW to begin.

Well, one day Tooty-Tooty Raccoon couldn't take it anymore: he got up the courage to knock on the Porcupine's door: He was afraid of getting hurt, but still wanted to try… to help out his neighbor who was quite out of line.

His love was stronger than his fear of getting hurt; so there he stood bravely in the dirt. His love gave him the courage to knock on the door. Would Pokey Pokey poke him in the nose? Or, would he see Tooty-Tooty's love, and want some more?

The door soon opened and there the Porcupine stood; Tooty-Tooty hoped he'd be quite understood.

"Pokey Pokey!" Tooty-Tooty shouted at the door:

WE PICKED YOU SOME GRAPES, AND WE CAN PICK MORE!"

"I would sure like to ask you if you don't mind….

WHY WON'T YOU BE KIND PORCUPINE?!"

Shelly and I would sure like to be

a part of your life, close, like family!"

"So, what do you say? Will you let us STAY?"

Tooty-Tooty asked Pokey Pokey that day.

The Porcupine thought a minute about how loving they were: He knew he had done nothing to deserve their kind deeds and words.

Then He exclaimed with his arms opened wide,

"OF COURSE YOU CAN STAY! COME ON INSIDE!"

"If Shelly wants to come, tell her it's okay. She doesn't have to hide behind the tree that way!"

"I have NEVER known love like this! So from now on I will protect my friends.

I won't just look out for myself anymore. I'm sorry for how I acted before!

I pray, "Dear Lord help me keep in mind... to be YOUR KIND PORCUPINE!

Instead of using my words, my hands, and my feet - to kick, or to slap, or to hurt when I speak:

Help me use these things in a powerful way, to make You happy GOD, and be KIND every day: in Jesus' Name, Amen.

Since Tooty Tooty stopped being afraid, and just thinking about himself, I can't even count all those he has helped. There have been so many, and Turtle Shelly changed too: when she stopped hiding behind trees, and started loving too. They are kind to everyone they meet!

And Pokey Pokey?

Well, let's see! He changed so much when he loved too. He was so happy he hardly knew what to do. Tooty-Tooty, and Turtle Shelly changed Pokey Pokey's name to, "Happy Belly."

He spent the rest of his life treating others like kin.

And guess what? It happened like he prayed: He learned how to be a GOOD FRIEND.

The Moral of the story is: You can't walk in love and fear at the same time! Walk in love and see how happy you become.

The End

The Rooster And The Cricket

(Knowing Our Purpose)

Once upon a time there lived a Cricket and a Rooster. Now, the Cricket had chirped all night long and was just about to go to sleep the next morning, when the Rooster let out with his early morning "Cocka-Doodle-Doo"

that woke up his WHOLE side of the world. The Cricket couldn't sleep, so went to the Rooster and said to him, "Why do you have to make such racket in the early hours the way you do?" To which the Rooster replied, "I have the morning shift, thank you very much. Hey! Why do you have to flap your wings and make that annoying sound ALL NIGHT and disturb my sleep?" Cricket said, "If you must know, I have the night shift, and so I'm just doing my job!" "Okay," said Rooster, "If you want to complain about MY singing then go right ahead, but I'll tell you what Mr. Smarty Pants, if you think I sing too loud then put yourself in MY place. Trade shifts with me and THEN see how you feel."

Cricket agreed, "Well, I don't really do morning's, but I guess it wouldn't hurt just this once."

Sure enough, that night the sun refused to go down because the Rooster wouldn't stop crowing. He got his cymbals out and he clanged and sang ALL NIGHT LONG! No one got any sleep on that whole side of the world the entire night.

The next morning, Cricket made his way to the top of the picket fence, tuned his violin and bellowed out the biggest song he could muster. As he sang "The Forest Anthem" the forest animals became outraged. "Why hasn't the sun gone down?" they began to ask each other (for this caused great disturbance in the natural course of things.) The coyotes were grumpy for they only hunt at night. That's when they see well. The possums and raccoons were all confused because they had only night vision also. "HEY!" shouted possum, "WILL SOMEBODY TURN OFF THE LIGHTS PLEASE?!"

The people in the town were cranky all day since no one got any sleep. The day shift had to work longer since day didn't end, and the night workers lost a whole night's pay since night never came.

"WHO IS TO BLAME FOR THIS?" they all began to question.

Rooster fessed up and told his side of the story: "It all started when Cricket COMPLAINED about my singing! I wanted the cricket to know what I go through, and to see very simply, no one can do my job LIKE I CAN."

Cricket stepped up and told his side: "Rooster is right! No one can wake the sunshine, but him. No one has a built-in alarm system, but him. I guess I thought I could do his job better than him because my song was better, but I can see clearly now, I have been given night ballads for a reason. I do apologize for getting this WHOLE side of the world in an uproar."

At that, every critter in the forest went to sleep, while the town's people waited for the sun to go down, and when it did, life could go on as usual.

Cricket had been up all day and was too tired to play his violin and sing all night; but he sang anyway till he couldn't sing anymore. He never wanted to go through that again!

Rooster slept sooo good all night and, was back to his old self by morning, and as usual, rose to the top of the picket fence and woke the sun, the farmer's and their families; he woke the town's people and their families too. He woke the cows for milking, the hogs for slopping, the bumble bees, and

EVEN THE DOG'S FLEAS.

Rooster and Cricket gained an appreciation for each other that day. An appreciation they never had before!

Now that things were back to normal, the farmers and their wives had been awake for SO many hours that when they FINALLY DID get to sleep, they snored SO loud, they even woke up their furry monkey slippers!!

The Moral of the story is: GOD made each of us on purpose, and for a purpose, His purpose. GOD is LOVE! Our purpose is to know Him and how very much He loves us, and to reveal Him everywhere we go! Let's do it!!

The End

The Unjust Judge

He pointed his finger, raised one brow, and jeered as he said, "You think you'll bear fruit, but how?"

He continued, "Why look at you! You are full of tangled vines, And yet you say you'll have more blooms this time?

Ha! That's the funniest thing I've heard yet!" The judge laughed out loud and would not relent.

He said to the tree, "All I see is a fruitless vine, weak and puney."

He sentenced the tree to a field alone: "Tree!" he said, "You will never beautify a home!"

She pleaded her case with the judge in the court: "Please, give me some time before you fill out your report. In two months I will be beautiful, you'll see. Then in your courtyard you'll want to plant me."

The Judge wouldn't hear any more from the tree. He said "This is absurd, what you are saying to me!"

He laughingly mocked with hysteria! But in two months the tree became a lovely Wisteria.

Friend! Do you want to be a Fireman, a Doctor, or a Nurse? Or, to take fresh water to someone who thirst?

Or, do you see yourself being a Bright Happy Clown, turning people's sad faces upside down?

Maybe you would like to plant flowers and trees; or to collect honey from the smart honeybees.

How would you like to work in a zoo with lions and hippos, and elephants too?

YOU can be all YOU imagine to be. If you think you can't… just remember this Tree.

The End

Why Do I Have To Be Different?

A Little Bird sat alone. He looked much different than the rest.
The other birds were active and strong, but he felt like he was so much less.
Little Bird often wondered why he couldn't be like them;
After all, they were all just little birds like him.
One morning some birds were playing hopscotch on the bird bath,
Little Bird watched them from a distance, and they would make him laugh.
O, how he wanted to play with them, and fly with them so bad;

But Little Bird only had one wing (Isn't that sad!)
Little Bird was rescued after a raccoon attacked him one night:
He had fallen from a tree into someone's campsite.
He was taken to a hospital. The Vet said he had nerve damage;
But at least he was alive and not the raccoon's sandwich! YIKES!!

Little Bird watched the other birds and enjoyed the games they'd play,
He was sure puzzled though and thought, "Why do I have to be this way?"
"I'm locked up in this big wire cage: will I ever FLY?

And, if I can't, why am I here? O WHY AM I?"
He said to himself, "I am so unimportant: I can't even play
and act like most of the other birds… why can't I anyway?

Suddenly and without warning to Little Bird at all,
A huge cat leaped onto the cage, and stared right into Little Bird's eyeball.
The cat licked his lips, then realized he could NOT get in.

The fur-ball put back his ears, and growled real loud at him.
Little Bird was thankful to GOD for sure from that day on
that he was being protected in his wire-caged Home!

When he stopped thinking about all he did NOT have,
He realized he COULD help on the bird bath. He asked if he could
keep score for them while they played their games:
The other birds were overjoyed, and they told him all their names.
They said they wanted to play games more often but they
couldn't find a scorekeeper.
Now that they found one in Little Bird, they chose to make him their Leader.

The Moral of the story is:
Everyone is different than somebody else; so why not go ahead and be yourself?!

The End

GOOD NEWS FLASH

The Monkey was fussing at the Kangaroo, "You just passed up all those bananas. What's the matter with you?

You could have stashed a bunch in your pocket... instead of hopping around and showing off your hip socket!"

Kangaroo replied, "My pocket is not for that!

It is a bed for my baby. He stays safe in my sack!"

Then the Parrot laughed at the Crow and said, "You haven't got any brains in your head.

I haven't heard you say ONE word!" Crow said, "That's because I'm not THAT kind of bird!"

A Porcupine criticized and said to the Aardvark, "Where are your spikes? You're not too sharp!"

"And why are you eating all those Ants? HA! Don't you know you'll get Ants in your pants?!"

Aardvark grumbled and said with a snort,

"Well, I don't know where you got your report; but I'm just doing what I'm supposed to do. That's what I'm supposing you do too."

So we learn from the animals one and all: GOD made some short & He made some TALL.

Don't look down on somebody else, just because they are not like yourself!!

One may be a Doctor, or you may be a Cook. You might
be an Author, or the Reader of a book.

Maybe one is a Methodist; another a Baptist;

One might be an Assembly of GOD; another could be a Catholic.

Maybe you can walk, or can't, and ride in a chair;

And you know everybody wears different underwear!

Simmer down and love like GOD does and get your act together;
because everybody on this earth is just as important as the other!
NO ONE IS BETTER!!

The End

The Ant And The Sloth

Once upon a time there lived a sloth in a tree
who looked down and saw the ant busy as could be.
Said the sloth to the ant, "Why don't you slow down?

I am tired just watching you working on the ground."
The busy ant had no time for any idle chat:
for he was busy building this and busy building that.
Pretty soon, he had built a home for his family,
while the sloth sat and watched from up there in the tree.

The sloth said to the ant, "Why work when you can rest?"
The ant replied, "Why not work when I can give my best?"
The sloth replied, "I'm protecting my good health and strong physique!"
The ant exclaimed, "I am strengthening myself, to carry you when you are weak!"
"You are eating all the leaves there in your tree,
when you should be preparing for winter, storing food for your family."
Said the sloth, "I would like to, really, that's a fact;

but, it takes so much energy to move around like that!"

So, come winter, when all the leaves had gone,
There was no food for sloth, nor did he have a home;
but underground a joyful sound was heard throughout the land.
Many came to greet and meet the Ant Family Band.
They were safe and happy and snuggly, all together,
all because one ant worked, and strengthened himself for the others.

Dear Reader, did you know GOD tells us about the ant in Proverbs chapter
6 of the bible? He tells us the ant is very small, but a very hard worker.

Help me take good care of myself and do my best Father GOD,
so I will be healthier and stronger for You, and so I can help
other people when they need it. In Jesus' Name Amen

The End

Tell Me Star

Star in the east can you hear my plea?
I wish you could speak to me?
Were you there that wonderful night
The angel appeared to the Shepherd's in white?

O tell me won't you please east star:
What it was like looking on from afar.
Did GOD give instructions to you to shine
Brighter for the Birth of our Savior divine?
What an honor to be chosen out of all the other stars!
He could have chosen to use the Moon or maybe even Mars.
O, what was it like? I'll ask if I may,
To guide the Shepherd's by night & by day?

Didn't you radiate through each valley and hill,
Knowing your purpose was being fulfilled?
O, I wished I had been there that glorious night!
But I'm glad you were, Star of light.

What was it like to witness the birth
Of our Beloved Savior from above the earth?
Won't you please tell me Star?!

The End

Sometimes I Cry

A nine year old girl wrote these words in her tablet: "Does anyone know how I feel?" When she was sad, or happy, or just wanted to talk about something, but didn't know who to tell, she would write a letter to GOD. She wrote all her thoughts to Him in her "Dear GOD" letters, just to get things off her chest. The girl is thirteen now, and says, "I still talk to GOD that way a lot of times, do you?" When I asked her why she writes letters to Him, she replied, "Sometimes I cry, and I don't even know why; but GOD knows why, so I just talk to Him, and I feel better when I write it down. GOD can handle my problems way better than I can, so I guess I'm giving them to Him when I do that!" "He can handle yours too!" the girl added.

I asked the young lady when did she start writing letters to GOD, and this is what she said: "Do your Mom and Dad ever argue, or fight? Mine did. My parents would argue and get really loud, and sometimes they would even hurt each other. Words sure can hurt too. When I was small, I would cry a lot, but no one knew except GOD. I wished I could have talked to Mom and Dad about them fighting so much, but I didn't know how.

Sometimes, I was afraid they would move apart from each other to different houses, and leave my brothers, and sister, and me. Other times, I wanted them to move apart from each other, so they would stop fussing so much! I felt guilty though for wanting my parents to live away from each other.

Some days and nights, I had too many feelings inside, like I was going to *POP*!!"

The young lady asked me, "Have you ever felt like this before? Like you would just *pop* if you didn't get some relief quick?" I told her I have felt like that lots of times. She wanted to tell me some more, so I just listened.

"So, that's why I just sat down and wrote GOD a letter, a lot of times from the backyard swing, and you know what? Something would happen, and still happens: after I write down all my feelings to Him, I guess He puts all of my problems in His suitcase, or somewhere, because I sure feel a lot better after I tell Him about them in a letter. All the knots in my stomach go away by the time I get to the end of my letter. Sometimes GOD doesn't help a person, because they don't want His help, but I do.

Then the young lady said to me, "You can write GOD a letter too, and He'll read it. You don't even have to mail it. If you don't write a letter, you can just talk to Him, and He won't tell anybody what you say."

When I asked this young lady what she did with her letters after she wrote them, she simply said, "I throw them away." That told me, GOD must really take away her burdens right away.

I can hardly wait to give the "GOD letters" a try. How about you?

The End

No Matter What

An unspoken promise is made between a sister and a brother during childhood. The unspoken promise is:

"I will love you no matter what!" Who will keep the promise, and who will not?

They did almost everything together: split the chores without complaining, made up stories together, built tents inside the house with sheets, blankets, and whatever else their Mom would allow. Lots of times, they pretended they were in some faraway place. One time, they even pretended they were astronauts, headed for the Moon, to find out once and for all if there really was a man in the Moon, and if there was any cheese on it. The day they visited the Moon in their imagination, the Sister snuck some cheese from the fridge in the kitchen ahead of time, so she could convince her younger Brother she broke it off the Moon.

Both of them loved to fish, and would every chance they could. Their Mama would tell them they could go after chores were done: "Just don't get in the water, unless I'm there with you!" she would say.

Tanner was the Brother, Lisa Faye was Sister's name. Brother Tanner just seemed to have a knack for fishing: it wasn't unusual for him to catch one after the other, and when they would catch enough for a meal, they would bring them home, Mama would clean them, and cook them up for supper. Daddy sure liked that! He was usually so tired after working all day; but once in a while, Daddy would play ball with Tanner, or Dad would help him with homework, while Lisa Faye and her Mama did the supper dishes, and got caught up on some sewing they had started.

The Mama and kids loved to sing together. Every once in a while, their Daddy would join in. Their parents and them loved family time and would spend it most evenings in the den playing games, or just being together.

Tanner and Lisa Faye would play together real well, most of the time; but sometimes they would get on each other's nerves and say some ugly, hurtful words to each other. Their Mama would tell them to forgive each other, and say they were sorry before going to sleep, because, you know what the Bible says: "Hurry and forgive before the sun goes down." The Weather Man on T.V. would say, "It's ten o'clock, do you know where your children are?" But Mama would say, "It's ten o'clock, time for bed: go brush your teeth, and make sure you forgive everybody, and say your prayers!"

Well, remember when I told you their Mama told them not to go in the lake without her being there? One Friday afternoon after school, and chores were done, Mama told Tanner, "You and your Sister go catch us some supper." Tanner thought he was going to catch a bunch of fish, one after the other, like usual, and he got this bright idea that if he went for a "quick swim" first, it would cool him down, and he could do a better job at catching them. At least, that's what he imagined anyway. He told Lisa Faye, "If I go swimming first, my clothes can dry out while I'm fishing afterwards." First, Tanner made his Sister promise not to tell on him, so she promised. "I won't tell on you for swimming, if you promise not to tell on me coz' I don't want to fish. I want to pick wild flowers for my collection at home."

They both agreed to keep quiet.

Well, on the third trip up the hill on the way to the rope that swings over the water, Tanner lost his balance. He fell and hurt his ankle really bad! There wasn't anything Lisa Faye could think to do except to run home to get Mama. When their Mama heard how Tanner had disobeyed her instructions, and found out there would be no fish for supper, Ooo wee, was Mama disappointed! After seeing and hearing how upset her Mama was over what Tanner had done, Lisa Faye didn't dare tell her Mama what she DIDN'T do: and that is, she didn't go fishing.

Their Mama had to ask a neighbor to drive them over to the lake where Tanner was, so they could drive him home. While Tanner was waiting for help to arrive, he made up another lie and told his Mama, "I was just about to catch probably the BIGGEST FISH IN THE WHOLE ENTIRE UNIVERSE, when that BIG FISH drug me into the water... I was barely hanging on to my pole for dear life! And that's when I fell and twisted my ankle!" Tanner told all of this to his Mama, thinking his Sister had kept quiet about him disobeying and going swimming. Now he was in double-trouble!!

After his Mama got him home, and wrapped his ankle, she had Tanner bend over the bathtub, and she gave him the time of his life. Just when his Sister thought she was off the hook, Tanner spilled the beans. Only thing is, he got his side of the story a little mixed up: "Mama" he said, Sister didn't want to fish, she wanted to pick wild flowers, and she asked me not to tell you, so while she picked flowers, I just decided to go swim is all." That's when Lisa Faye spoke up in her defense and told their Mama she wouldn't dare have disobeyed "If Brother hadn't thought of it first!" she blurted out. Guess what? They both got a much needed spanking after that.

Now, the sister forgave her brother; but the Brother?
Hmm, he just wouldn't let it go.

Anytime he and Lisa Faye had a disagreement after that, Tanner would bring up her "ratting" on him as he called it. He didn't understand. His sister just wanted to get him help. That's all she was thinking about. She didn't think about how it would hurt her brother's trust in her.

The next few days, Tanner and his sister didn't spend much time together. It seemed like they had lost the friendship they had for so long. Both of them had their feeling's hurt.

Lisa didn't know how to help her brother trust her again. She missed their closeness. Tanner used that to his advantage. He started manipulating his sister into doing his chores, and to give him part of her allowance. He would make her think she needed to pay him back for telling on him.

No matter how much Lisa Faye did for Tanner, it never seemed to be enough. It was like, the more she did for him, the worse he got. He wasn't forgiving his sister. He wasn't forgetting what she did, and wouldn't let her forgive herself either. Finally, Lisa Faye got so tired of her brother treating her so unkindly, she was beginning to be angry at him for not forgiving her. Now Lisa Faye needed to forgive Tanner!

The parents noticed their children weren't getting along like before. The Mom and Dad prayed about it and GOD helped them to know what to do. The parents called the kids in the room.

Their Dad started the conversation: "Kids, I want to tell you a story, then I want you to tell me what the end should be, okay?" They agreed.

"A man had two sons." he said. One son was caught telling a lie after he stole a kid's lunch money at school. After stealing it, he said he didn't do it. Also, he said he went to school the day before, but that wasn't true either. He spent the day fishing all day instead. Not only that, but rather than doing his chores his Dad gave him to do, his Dad caught him bullying his brother to do them. On top of that, he bullied him to give up his allowance to him too. When the Daddy was about to punish his son for all the wrongs he did, and lies he told, the man's son got on his knees, and cried. He cried BIG CROCODILE TEARS too, and begged his Daddy to give him another chance to do the right thing. The boy cried, "I'm so so sorry Dad! Please forgive me and don't punish me!!!!"

The Daddy felt sorry for his son, changed his mind, and said, "I forgive you Son! Now go, and don't do it again!" His son thanked him.

Immediately, the same son went and found his brother who stole his allowance and never paid it back.

He held his brother down on the floor so he couldn't move, and put his hand over his brother's mouth, and told him, "Give me ALL your allowance you have saved up, or I'm telling Mom and Dad you stole mine... and you will be punished!"

The brother cried, and he cried, and cried. When the mean boy took his hand off his brother's mouth, the boy couldn't hardly speak because he was crying so hard. The younger brother said, "I don't have any money! Please please forgive me and give me till Friday and I'll give you all my allowance then, I promise!" Their Dad overheard his son crying, and came running in to the boy's room to help, just in time to see his one Son that he had just forgiven a lot of stuff – holding down the other one. When the Dad found out the son who had been forgiven A LOT, was not forgiving the one who had done little, he was angry!!

Now the Dad telling the story, asked Tanner and Lisa Faye,
"What do you think this Dad should do about his sons?"

Immediately, Tanner shouted out, "Punish him, and take away all his stuff, AND make him give his own allowance for a whole month to his brother he bullied!"

With sadness in his eyes, Tanner's Dad replied, "Is that what I should do with you Son: Give a whole month of your allowance to your sister? That is what you have been doing to her by not forgiving her."

By now, their Mom and Dad were both in tears as they explained to their children the story Jesus told when He said, "For if you don't forgive someone of their wrongs, your Father in Heaven will not forgive you of your wrongs."

Now, Tanner and Lisa were crying, as they realized their love
for each other, and how THEY ALMOST GAVE IT UP!

Lisa Faye said to Tanner, "Now do you forgive me Brother?" Brother replied, "I'm the one Sis, who needs to ask your forgiveness. I am so sorry for how I have treated you!" Afterward, Tanner & Lisa Faye apologized to their Mom for lying to her! Lisa Faye forgave her brother, and their Mom forgave them both.

Tanner added, "Sister, whatever happens in our whole life, let's promise each other right now, we will always forgive each other before we go to sleep… like Mama always says. And, we will keep on loving each other,

NO MATTER WHAT!!"

The Moral of this story is: Do not delay, forgive today!

The End

Credits

I dedicate this book to all my readers. For whatever reason you stopped by, Thank You!

My son, Dwight gave me the name "Psalma Mama."

"I have been so very blessed to have a story telling mama. She not only reads encouraging words and bedtime stories, but writes them too. Like the songs of Psalms, her writings have touched so many lives. That's why I've named her Psalma Mama. " –Dwight Gwin

When I was my dirtiest, when I was at my worst, GOD found me, loved me out of the mess I was in. Jesus lived and died and rose again for me. That's why I thank Him first; because He gifted me to write, and I can't help but tell about it. He did all of this for you too.

My deep heart appreciations go to my husband, George for his patience the whole last day of getting all these images organized and sent for publishing. Thank you George for sticking it out with me, and working long hours to help bring this to completion!

To Amy Tavares for using her editing skills for many of the stories, and for sacrificing long hours to help find just the right images for a few of the stories.

To Henry, for his daily prayers and editing support, along with his daily Scriptures of encouragement that I have come to see as "morning dew" for my soul.

I would like to thank Jon Lineback and Gwen Ash of West Bow Press for their kind and patient spirit on the phone always. Thank you Jon for the idea to write a story called "Chocolate Chip Morsels," after I titled the book that. I had fun writing that story, after asking the Lord for the creative ideas for it. He gave them too.

Thank you to all my friends for your prayers and patient understanding when I have to say, "No" to our enjoyable luncheons and sing-a-longs, so I can stay in and listen to the Lord better.

Images for "Under GOD's Love" were drawn and colored by my very creative granddaughter, Erin Olivia Otts. Other images throughout the book were provided by BigStock.com, and 123rf.com.

*Cinderella rhyme in "The Day I Met GOD" is public domain.

Dawn's biography

Dawn Gwin is a mother of four children: two boys and two girls. She and her husband, George have ministered to children of all ages and cultures for more than 30 years. She is an accomplished prolific writer of stories, songs, poems, devotions, puppet scripts, and skits. Dawn is a chaplain at the local hospital, local jail, and is involved in teaching weekly bible class at the local prison. Dawn has three cd's: "Still Waters;" "Come Away To My Love;" and "Uniting Generations." She attributes all the glory to the grace of GOD.

Printed in the United States
By Bookmasters